The Case of the Cannabis Cat

William Jenkins

i

THE CASE OF THE CANNABIS CAT

The Case of the Cannabis Cat

Published by
William Jenkins
4036 Pine Street
Burnaby BC V5G 1Z5
Canada
williamhenryjenkins@gmail.com
http://www.editingservicesbilljenkins.ca
Telephone: 1-778-928-6139

The cover design is courtesy of Laura Shinn, Author and Book Cover Designer & Formatter.

THE CASE OF THE CANNABIS CAT

.

Table of Contents

Chapter 1 Discussing the Law

The Frayne family live in a two-storey house in Brockville, Ontario a few blocks from Winston Churchill Public School where Tommy is in Grade Five and Terry is in Grade Two. The house has a center-hall plan with the living room on one side, the dining room and, behind it, the kitchen, on the other side.

Usually, they eat in the dining room, but tonight they are sitting around the kitchen table. The more casual area encourages conversation and that is exactly what is going on.

Tommy and his three close friends, Mary, Dick and Bobby formed a Private Investigator's Club to solve mysteries that occur in their lives. They like the idea of being able to figure out what has happened whether the event is a crime, a natural disaster or just a family mystery.

Tommy's father is a car mechanic, not a lawyer, so when Tommy starts asking about police procedures, he has to rely on his experience, various TV shows and general knowledge. He is not embarrassed to say "I don't know" when he doesn't know the answer.

"Suppose we were private detectives, solving a crime; could the police stop us from investigating? Tommy asks.

"Sure," says his father. "They can seal up the crime scene, put tape around the area and say that no one is allowed to come closer than the tape."

Photo courtesy John Lehman Globe and Mail

1

"Would they arrest us if we went beyond the tape?"

"Not likely. They would probably just tell you to get out."

"Are they going to arrest Tommy?" asks Terry.

"Not if he doesn't break the law," replies her mother. "He is just asking about what the rules are so that he doesn't break them."

"Anyway," says his father, "if they arrest you, they give you a warning."

"I know about that," says Tommy. He quotes the Miranda warning "You have the right to remain silent. Anything you say can and will be used against you in a court of law. You have the right to speak to an attorney, and to have an attorney present during any questioning. If you cannot afford a lawyer, one will be provided for you at government expense."

"You have been watching TV," says his father. "That's the warning for the United States. In Canada, they don't warn you about keeping silent. That is a right that you have from the Charter of Rights and Freedom, part of the Canadian Constitution. They are more likely to say "What happened here?" or "Can you explain what happened?" Actually, in Canada, you have the right to contact a lawyer to ask him questions and retain him but the police are not required to let him attend the interview. If you decide not to say anything, you simply say "My lawyer will speak for me" and keep silent otherwise."

Photo courtesy iStockphoto

"Wow!" says Tommy. "I guess it's best just to keep silent."

"Definitely. Now in England, it's a little different. In England the police say that if you don't tell us something now when we are asking you about it, you won't be able to bring it up later as part of your defense. That's a much tougher situation because it means you had better talk now."

British Police

"What happens if it's a company? They can't arrest a company, can they?"

"Well," says his father, "I don't know about that. Probably your uncle Roger could tell you because he's a detective and gets involved in things like that. They have laws about gangs and criminal organizations but how they handle it, I don't know."

His mother commented "Some of the gangs sell illegal drugs like marijuana, heroin or cocaine. Other gangs do extortion. That is, they tell a store owner to pay them so much a week or else they will burn down their store. Some gangs bring people here illegally for a fee. Many organizations violate the laws."

Terry asks "Does Uncle Roger catch the gangs?"

"He tries to," says her mother. "It's a hard job."

"I'd like to be a detective when I grow up," says Tommy. "I like solving mysteries."

Tommy went off to his room to work on some homework and Terry went out to find a friend and practice her skipping.

"Tommy seems quite interested in legal matters," says his mother.

"Yes," his father replies. "I wonder if he realizes how complicated the law can be."

Chapter 2 The Next Mystery

Every day, when she is finished work, Mrs. Frayne picks up Terry after school and walks home with her. Brockville is a safe city and the walk is only a few blocks from school to home but Mrs. Frayne doesn't want anything bad to happen to Terry so she takes the time to walk home with her.

The next afternoon, as the two arrive home, a taxi pulls up and the driver says "I have a package for Tommy Frayne. Does he live here?"

They accept the package, a box about two feet long and a foot by a foot in width and depth. Tommy's mother carries the box into the house and takes it up to Tommy's room. She asks Terry to remind her of the parcel when Tommy gets home.

A few minutes later a bouncy Tommy Frayne charges in the house, throws some books on the couch in the living room and shouts "I have to go to a meeting of PIC at Mary's house."

His mother calls "There's a parcel for you in your room, dear."

"I'll get it later," he calls and off he runs.

The PIC is holding a meeting to discuss a new case. At Mary's house, the four detectives drink some lemonade and talk about possible mysteries to solve. They have heard that someone broke a window at a house on Mary's street. Also, there was a robbery in a house near Bobby's but the only thing stolen was a cell phone and some cash that had been on a dresser in the bedroom. Finally Bobby brings up the fact that something is causing circular blotches on some lawns where the grass is dying.

Blotches on lawn

After some discussion, they decide to look into the circular blotches. Dick thinks that they could be caused by extra-terrestrials shining a laser beam on the lawns from a flying saucer hovering over Brockville. The others are more conventional.

"I suspect it is some form of fungus that is attacking the grass," says Mary. "We should take samples and see if we can grow the bacteria ourselves."

"I bet it is caused by pets peeing on the lawn," says Bobby.

"Don't be vulgar," says Mary.

Tommy agrees to approach someone with blotches on his lawn and ask if he can take a small sample for analysis. Dick seems to think it happens at night and that they should sit up overnight near one of the blotches and watch for space ships.

Bobby says "This is stupid. Why don't we find some real mysteries to solve? I think we need a change in leadership. It's time I took over as President so we can start doing something really worthwhile."

Mary argued that she was appointed for three mysteries and would hand the presidency over when the third one is solved.

"Great!" says Bobby. "I'll get to be president just after the space invaders land."

"That might be soon," says Dick.

The meeting ended with no change in management of PIC.

Chapter 3 A Real Mystery

The kids head home for supper and, at last, Tommy looks at his package. He notices that the address is Tommy Frayne, PIC; so he thinks the box might contain a mystery for the Club to solve. He notices the small holes in the side of the box, big enough for a pencil to slip through.

His sister, Terry, comes to his room and asks him what is in the box and Tommy says, "Let's find out."

He opens the box and out pops a cat. It is black and white, a male, an adult cat with a harness that goes around its neck and shoulders. Hanging from the harness is a little barrel, something like the one a St. Bernard rescue dog would have, but much smaller.

Terry is delighted and runs to tell their mother. Tommy carries the cat into the kitchen and they set a saucer of milk down for the cat to drink.

Boy with a cat

Tommy does not find a note in the package and no indication as to who sent it.

"What will we name the cat?" asks Terry.

"I think we should call it 'Miss Terry'" says Tommy. Terry objects saying it would be confusing. Tommy points out that he has made a joke, a pun, because the cat is a mystery. He explains that a pun is a humorous play on words. "See: Miss Terry and mystery!" he says.

They discuss the cat and its unusual harness and barrel. When father gets home, they have supper and have to make some decisions about the cat.

Chapter 4 The Police Arrive

They are finished supper and Tommy and Terry do the dishes while they discuss the cat. They decide that it is a house cat, not a wild one. They will let it go anywhere inside the house. However, they are afraid to let the cat outside, because it might run away so they talk about using a leash.

"We should get a sand box for him," says Tommy. "We can put it in the kitchen."

Tommy phones Mary and tells her about the cat.

"It came in a parcel addressed to PIC. It's a mystery," he says.

She promises to tell Dick and Tommy about the cat. "Maybe we'll make him our mascot," she says.

There is a knock on the door and Father lets in Constable Bidwell. He says he has information about illegal drugs in the house and he wants to speak with all the family. Everyone sits down in the living room and Bidwell asks Tommy, "Do you have any illegal drugs here?"

Officer Bidwell

Tommy replies, "I'm sorry, Mr. Bidwell, but I cannot

say anything. My lawyer will speak for me."

He tries Terry, who gives the same response.

He turns to the adults and they too say that their lawyer will speak for them but they mention their Charter Rights and don't have to say anything.

Bidwell says "I'm afraid you will all have to come with me" and he parades them out and into a squad car.

Tommy points out that he can't leave his new cat unattended. Bidwell goes back, sees the box with the PIC address, and brings out the cat and box.

Chapter 5 A Free Ride to the Station

The ride to the Police Station was rather eventful. Constable Bidwell drove quickly and had the siren going the whole way. The Frayne's stared at each other but didn't say a word.

At the Police Station, the four, complete with cat, are placed in an interview room. Father cautions everyone to keep silent as the police may be recording everything they say.

Brockville Police Station

Tommy says "We didn't do anything wrong. I'm going to be my own lawyer."

The police take Tommy into a different interview room and he agrees to act as his own lawyer. He is asked about PIC.

"The PIC is a club formed to solve mysteries," Tommy says.

The police get the names of the other club members and soon they are all together in an interview room.

Constable Bidwell explains that he opened the barrel hanging around the cat's neck and found a substance that looks surprisingly like marijuana.

"The substance has been sent to the lab for analysis," says Constable Bidwell. "We think it is an illegal drug and the cat is being used to distribute illegal drugs around the city," he says.

Constable Bidwell explains "Since the cat belongs to PIC, the Club President is considered to be the person of authority and can be prosecuted for possession of an illegal drug, leader of an organization intent on criminal activity and probably guilty of trafficking in illegal drugs, for which the maximum sentence is life imprisonment."

There is a stunned silence for about 30 seconds and then all four say "I have nothing to say. My lawyer will speak for me."

The police ask who is the President of the Club and Mary admits to it; however, she offers Bobby the chance to be President now. He declines.

The police ask Tommy if he is prepared to be the lawyer for all the club members. He agrees but says "We have nothing to say at the moment."

Chapter 6 Interrogation

Constable Bidwell is interrupted by a message saying "We now know who sent the package to the PIC. It was Tommy's great grandfather, Captain Thomas, and he is in the other room, confessing to having the cat and box delivered to Tommy's house. The police suggest that this criminal organization is a family affair, spanning four generations.

Tommy says "I cannot speak for Captain Thomas."

Constable Bidwell turns on Dick, calling him "Richard". He points out "Richard, you are equally guilty of possession of the illegal substance as a member of the organization and besides, the President reported to you that the cat had been safely delivered to the Vice-President's home. Thus, you are guilty of possession, even though you weren't at the house, and hadn't seen the cat or marijuana. You are liable for a sentence of 14 years in prison."

Everyone looked at Richard and he said "My lawyer will speak for me".

Finally, Constable Bidwell turns to Bobby and asks how he would like to spend 14 years in prison. Does he wish to confess to these crimes? The court will deal less harshly with someone who provides the evidence so he could get off with just probation if he explains what is really going on.

Bobby, who has no clue as to what is going on, says "My lawyer will speak for me."

The police conclude they aren't going to get anywhere so they announce they will hold all the kids in jail for a few months while they await trial.

Mary then announces that she has decided to fire her lawyer and will act in her own defense. Tommy says "Lots of luck. You have a fool for a client."

Mary says "Possession requires me to know what I

possess. Beaver vs. Regina 1957. Since none of us knew what was in the cat's drum, none of us is guilty of possession."

> **Beaver v. The Queen [1957]** is a leading decision of the <u>Supreme Court of Canada</u> on the <u>mens rea</u> requirement in criminal law to prove "possession". The Court held that an offence based on possession, such as possession of a narcotic, requires the <u>Crown</u> to prove that the accused had subjective knowledge of the nature of the object in possession.

"But," the police reply, "how do we know that you knew what we know?"

Mary replies "I know that you think that you know what we knew but no one knew what you think you now know."

The police are rather puzzled by this statement and all they can say is a rather weak "We know".

There is a knock on the door of the interview room and in walks Tommy's uncle, Detective Roger Edwards. "What is going on here?" he asks.

Officer Bidwell says, "We have interrupted a major criminal organization trafficking in illegal drugs and we are interviewing the main suspects."

Chapter 7 Innocent Until Proven Guilty

"Outside," says Detective Edwards to Constable Bidwell. They go out, leaving the four criminals alone.

"How did you know the law about possession?" asked Tommy.

"I have a copy of the Criminal Code of Canada," says Mary. "The precedent is one of the cases related to possession."

"Do you know the whole Criminal Code?"

"I know most. I figured it would be useful in our PIC to know what the law says."

"How are we going to get out of this mess?" asks Dick.

"They don't really have a case," says Mary. "You were wise to keep silent. That usually causes a lot of trouble if you admit anything at all."

"All we can admit," says Bobby "is we don't know what's going on."

"First of all," says Mary, "we are presumed to be innocent of any wrongdoing until there has been a trial and we are found guilty. A basic fact of Canadian justice is the presumption of innocence."

> Section 11(d) of the Canadian Charter of Rights and Freedom provides that any person charged with an offence has the right to be presumed innocent until proven guilty according to law in a fair and public hearing by an independent and impartial tribunal.

Extract from the Canadian Charter of Rights and Freedom

Bobby says "Constable Bidwell doesn't think I'm innocent. He keeps talking about 14 years in jail."

"But he is just investigating," says Mary. "Even if we are charged with anything, we aren't guilty until a trial is over and a jury listens to the whole story and decides on our innocence or guilt. If they find us innocent, that's the end of it. If guilty, the judge may even just give us suspended sentences so we may not go to jail at all."

Tommy says, "I thought that any questioning of a minor had to be done in the presence of his parent. Why were they questioning us without our parents being here?"

Mary says "I think this is all one big spoof. Everyone is in on this charade. I bet your Captain Thomas is behind all this. He's the one who sent us the cat. And anyway, the Criminal Code is quite clear on people of our age. We cannot be convicted of an offense which occurred when we were under the age of twelve. I guess only Bobby can go to jail because the rest of us are only ten."

"Oh oh", says Bobby. "So I'm the fall guy! That's the problem with being more mature than the rest of you."

"I know," whispers Richard. "I bet they are all watching us on TV. Let's pretend to be fighting and see what they do."

Wrestling

So the kids start wrestling around and, as expected, within a few minutes, Bidwell and Edwards are back in the room breaking up the fight.

Chapter 8 Getting Off with a Smile

"Okay," says Mary. "The game has gone on long enough. I have some homework to do tonight. Tell everyone it was a good joke but I have to head home now."

The kids were led out of the interview room and found the Fraynes and the police chief sitting around having a coffee. Terry was in an easy chair, petting the cat. There was no sign of Captain Thomas.

"Well," says the Chief, "things were pretty quiet around here so we thought we'd have some fun with the Private Investigators Club. How did you like your introduction to police work?"

Police Chief

"It was interesting," says Mary. "I wonder if we could charge all you adults with conspiracy."

Bobby says "You had me fooled."

Richard and Tommy agree. It was a mystery because we really didn't know how much trouble we were in when we hadn't done anything wrong.

"Luckily for you boys, your President knows something about the Criminal Code," says the Chief.

Everyone is driven home in marked police cars but at least the sirens aren't on.

Appendix 1 Published Books

The **Private Investigator Club** stories are available as individual paperback books and as eBooks. A list of available stories is available on the website http://www.editingservicesbilljenkins.ca/jenkins.

Note that the publishing services are free. If you have written a story, poem or play and would like to have it published on Amazon or Kindle, contact William Jenkins by email address.

William Jenkins

Appendix 2 Overview of The Case of the Diligent Detectives

The Case of the Diligent Detectives begins with Bobby running the meeting. It is his turn to be President. He wants the young detectives to become more diligent in their investigations. He overrules various suggestions for investigation and chooses investigating the brown blotches that are appearing on the grass. He suspects that alien spacecraft are hovering over the city at night and shining powerful laser beams at the ground, thereby causing the death of the grass in various places. He decides that he needs to sit in a pup tent in the park and take photos of any flying saucers that come by. The others agree to investigate but decide to trick him by building a small flying saucer that they can float over his tent. Dick builds the device and paints his hockey mask green. He gets dressed in green pajamas. After dark, the three conspirators arrive in front of Bobby's tent and start making alien noises. The trick backfires. Bobby is not amused. The next night, to make up for their insubordination, the three other detectives camp out and investigate diligently. What happens has to be read to be believed. The story provides an opportunity for the reader to learn Morse code, a little French and the unexplained mysteries of aliens who come in the night.

www.ingramcontent.com/pod-product-compliance
Lightning Source LLC
Chambersburg PA
CBHW071230130626
46555CB00004B/1929